This book was written for my son, James Daniel. May you always make mistakes and never be afraid to fix them.

Pocket was a kangaroo who loved to go shopping.

James liked to go too, they went shopping and HOPPING!

James was just a little guy so they shopped with his mama.

They always made a list so there wasn't any drama.

James and Pocket each added
items to the list.

When they went to the store,
they found things real swift.

When they walked through the aisles, they found it very tough.

Cause they looked and they looked and they wanted ALLLLLL the stuff!

I want this, I want that, I want
this, and that too!

They grabbed so many things
they didn't know what to do.

"OH I KNOW! The things that we want, lets put in my pouch."

"When we are done shopping, we'll meet mom to check out."

James skipped, Pocket hopped,
they got so many things.

Avocados, watermelon, chips,
and green beans.

They dropped it all in, then they
went to find mommy.

They hopped all down the aisles,
and James slipped on salami!

Pocket found mommy and she picked James right up.

She said, "I'm sorry you're hurt, and I love you so much."

Hand in hand they all went to pay
for their food.

Everyone was in such a great
mood.

In all the commotion, they didn't remember......

...they had stuffed Pocket's pouch with what they wanted for dinner!

They got to the car and they
quickly realized.

Mommy said, "that's ok, we all
make mistakes sometimes"

Pocket, James, and Mommy took
it all back inside the store.

They apologized and helped
return the items to the floor.

"I'm proud of you," said mommy.
Being honest is so hard and so is
sticking to a list.

Next time we will remember to
write down the things you
missed.

'It's important to be honest no matter what people think of you".

"Doing the right thing makes you feel better too!"

James and Pocket agreed they would always try to be honest.

Doing the right thing feels great.
Try it, we promise!

The End

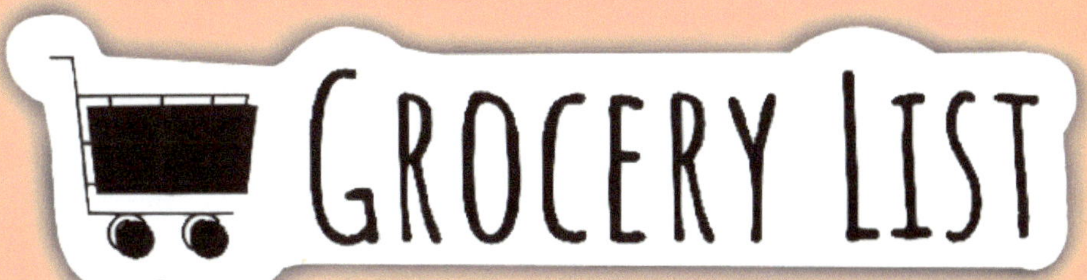

How to correct my mistakes

1. Acknowledge that I made a mistake
2. Tell myself "It's okay, I can fix it."
3. Think of ways to fix it.
4. If I don't know what to do, ask someone I trust for help.
5. Fix the mistake and move on.

Mistakes are
how we learn.

Find the author on instagram @mrs_cassandra_clark